Tippy
the
Fox Terrier

Tippy
the
Fox Terrier

by
Cynthia Overbeck

CAROLRHODA BOOKS
MINNEAPOLIS, MINNESOTA U.S.A

Revised English text by Cynthia Overbeck. Original French text by Anne-Marie Pajot. Translation by Dyan Hammarberg. Photographs by Claudine Marechal. Drawings by L'Enc Matte.

LIBRARY OF CONGRESS CATALOGING IN PUBLICATION DATA

Overbeck, Cynthia
Tippy, the fox terrier.

(The Animal Friends Books)
Original ed. published under title: Chipie la petite chienne.
SUMMARY: Describes the life of a fox terrier that lives in an apartment building in the city.

1. Fox terriers—Juvenile literature. [1. Fox terriers. 2. Dogs]
I. Pajot, Anne Marie. Chipie la petite chienne. II. Maréchal,
Claudine Huza. III. Matte, L'Enc. IV. Title.

SF429.F509 1976   636.7′55   76-1230
ISBN 0-87614-071-1

First published in the United States of America 1976 by
Carolrhoda Books, Inc. All English language rights reserved.

Original edition published by Librairie A. Hatier, Paris,
France, under the title CHIPIE LA PETITE CHIENNE.
English text and drawings © 1976 Carolrhoda Books, Inc.
Photographs © 1974 Librairie A. Hatier.

Manufactured in the United States of America.
Published simultaneously in Canada by J. M. Dent & Sons
(Canada) Ltd., Don Mills, Ontario.

International Standard Book Number: 0-87614-071-1
Library of Congress Catalog Card Number: 76-1230

For children all over the world, dogs are very special playmates and friends. Tippy, the playful little dog in this book, is a friend of Peter and his younger sister, Alison. Tippy first came to live with them when she was a tiny puppy. As she grew up, she and the children spent many hours playing together. And now that Tippy is full-grown, she's like one of the family.

Tippy is a wire-haired fox terrier. She has a thick, fluffy coat and bushy whiskers. Her eyebrows are so long that they almost cover her bright

black eyes. Early this summer, the children took these snapshots of Tippy. She certainly seemed to know that her picture was being taken!

Tippy lives with Alison and Peter in their parents' apartment, high above the city. In the daytime, the little dog likes to stand on the balcony and watch the people and the cars that go by in the street below. At night, she sleeps indoors. She has her own bed—a straw basket with a soft cushion. She has her own dishes, too, and a set of toys to play with.

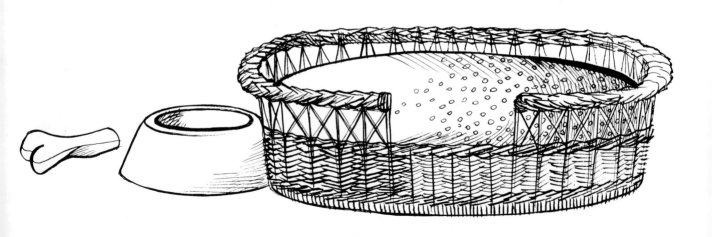

Except for the outdoor walks that she likes to take, Tippy spends most of her time in the house. But her ancestors were not house pets—they were hunting dogs. Long ago in England, fox terriers were trained to hunt foxes and rabbits. The terriers dug into these animals' underground hiding places and chased the creatures out into the open. Often, too, farmers trained terriers to dig out and kill the mice and rats that lived in their homes and fields.

Nowadays, most terriers do not hunt. They are house pets, like Tippy. But other kinds of dogs, such as setters, retrievers, and pointers, are both hunting dogs and pets. These dogs help their owners to hunt ducks, geese, and other wild birds. They are smart, energetic dogs, and they can learn to obey complicated commands. Because they are so lively and intelligent, they also make good household pets.

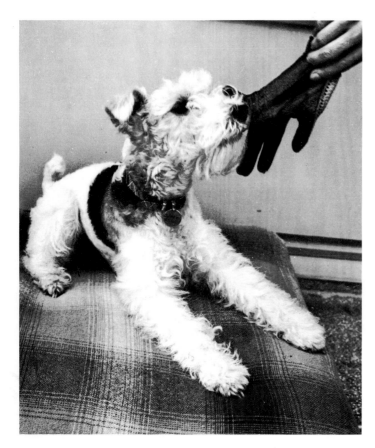 

Like her hunting relatives, Tippy is a smart and playful dog. Sometimes she gets a little *too* playful. Today, she has gotten hold of a brand new glove to chew on. She holds it tightly in her mouth, and she growls and shakes her head from side to side.

When the children's mother tries to pull the glove out of Tippy's mouth, the little dog acts as though it's a game. She gets so excited that she barks and wags her tail at the same time.

After all this excitement, Tippy decides that it's time for a snack. She heads for her special corner of the kitchen, where there are two dishes— one for food, and one for water. Alison and Peter see to it that there's always clean water in one dish. They put a fresh supply of dried or canned dog food in the other dish twice a day.

Tippy gobbles her food quickly. Afterwards she laps up water, a few drops at a time, with her long tongue.

Although Tippy has had a busy morning, Peter and Alison want her to play with them a little longer. They take her up to the roof of the apartment building, where it's sunny and warm. But the summer sun is too hot for Tippy, and she doesn't feel like playing. So she chooses a comfortable chair where she can rest.

Soon, she's so hot that her tongue hangs out of her mouth, and she pants as if she's out of breath. Like all dogs, Tippy pants in order to cool herself off when she's too warm. She has sweat glands in her skin and on the bottoms of her feet. But she cools off mostly by breathing in extra air through her mouth.

"Poor Tippy! She looks so miserable," says Peter. "Maybe a haircut would make her feel better. Her coat is so long and shaggy—it must make her very hot."

The children's mother agrees with Peter. She asks the children to take Tippy for a haircut. So Peter and Alison put a leash on Tippy and start off down the street. But it looks as though Tippy has her own ideas about where she wants to go. She pulls and tugs on her leash, and she finally stops right in the middle of the sidewalk.

"Look, Peter," says Alison, "it's almost as if she knows where we're taking her. She doesn't like haircuts any more than you do!"

"Maybe she'd rather run around on her own and explore," says Peter.

But Peter and Alison know that it's dangerous to let Tippy run loose—she might get hit by a car. So they keep a tight hold on her leash, even though she doesn't like it.

Finally, the children manage to get Tippy to the Pet Center. Inside, there are all kinds of dogs, from fancy toy poodles to giant St. Bernards. They're all getting their coats washed and clipped, and their toenails trimmed. Some of them are even having ribbons tied in their fur.

Tippy gets a bath and a haircut—nothing fancy. But when she comes out of the shop, she looks so clean and neat! She seems to feel better, too. Now she doesn't even mind the leash, and she's ready and eager to take a walk with Alison and Peter.

As the three of them walk along, Tippy keeps her nose close to the ground, taking in all the smells. She has a very good sense of smell, and she can recognize objects just by their odor. If she found one of Alison's hair ribbons on the ground, for example, she would know it belonged to Alison because of its familiar smell. Tippy's sense of smell also tells her whether a cat has passed by recently, or whether there's a tasty bit of food nearby.

With so many interesting things to smell, Tippy is enjoying her walk. It gives her the exercise she needs, too. She has lots of energy, and Peter and Alison must walk her every day, even when the weather gets cold.

Tippy won't mind the cold, because she has a beautiful new red coat to wear this winter. It will keep her warm and dry, even when there's snow outside.

Alison and Peter are proud of Tippy. "With her haircut and her new red coat," says Alison, "Tippy is the prettiest dog in the whole city!"

DO YOU KNOW . . .

- how many different kinds of dogs there are?

- why dogs often lick their noses?

- what kind of dog is only five inches tall?

TO FIND THE ANSWERS TO THESE QUESTIONS, TURN THE PAGE ☞

FACTS ABOUT DOGS

Dogs belong to the group of mammals—warm-blooded animals that nurse their babies.

All dogs are *carnivorous* (kar-NIV-er-us); they eat mostly meat.

Dogs are color blind, which means that they cannot tell one color from another. They must pick out an object by its movement, by its brightness, or by its shape, instead of by its color.

The ancestors of the dog were probably the first animals in history to be domesticated, or tamed, by humans. Thousands of years ago, cave people trained wild wolves and jackals to protect them and to help them hunt. All modern domestic dogs are descended from these first tame wolves and jackals.

Wolf

Jackal

Dogs have good hearing and a good sense of smell. Their sense of smell is sharpest when their noses are wet: this is why dogs often lick their noses.

Most dogs have 2 coats of hair on their bodies: an outer coat, which protects the dog from rain and snow, and an undercoat, which keeps the dog warm. In winter, the undercoat grows thick; in summer it is shed.

There are about 200 different breeds, or kinds, of domestic dogs. These dogs come in all shapes and sizes, from tiny chihuahuas to huge Irish wolfhounds.

Chihuahua
1-6 lb. (0.5-2.7 kg)
5 in. (13 cm)

Irish Wolfhound
105-140 lb. (48-64 kg)
30-34 in. (76-86 cm)

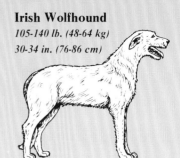

Of the 200 breeds of dogs, 21 are terriers. The dog in this book is a wire-haired fox terrier. The pictures below show 4 other kinds of terriers.

Skye Terrier

Scottish Terrier

Airdale Terrier

Manchester Terrier

A mother dog usually gives birth to a litter of 1 to 12 puppies at a time. When the puppies are born, they are blind, deaf, and helpless. They open their eyes 10 to 12 days after birth. Puppies drink their mother's milk until they are 4 or 5 weeks old; then they begin to eat solid food.

The average dog lives about 13 years. A 2-year-old dog can be compared in age to a 24-year-old human. After a dog's second year, each year of its life is like 4 years of a person's life. So a 13-year-old dog could be compared in age to a 68-year-old person.

The Animal Friends Books

Clover the CALF
Jessie the CHICKEN
Ali the DESERT FOX
Splash the DOLPHIN
Dolly the DONKEY
Downy the DUCKLING
ELEPHANTS around the World
Tippy the FOX TERRIER
Marigold the GOLDFISH
Polly the GUINEA PIG
Winslow the HAMSTER
Figaro the HORSE

Rusty the IRISH SETTER
Boots the KITTEN
Penny and Pete the LAMBS
The LIONS of Africa
Mandy the MONKEY
Lorito the PARROT
Curly the PIGLET
Whiskers the RABBIT
Shelley the SEA GULL
Penelope the TORTOISE
Sprig the TREE FROG
Tanya the TURTLE DOVE

CAROLRHODA BOOKS
241 FIRST AVENUE NORTH — MINNEAPOLIS, MINNESOTA 55401

Published in memory of Carolrhoda Locketz Rozell,
Who loved to bring children and books together

Please write for a complete catalogue